NEVER UNDERESTIMATE A HERMIT CRAB

Written and illustrated by
Daniel Sean Kaye

THIS BOOK IS DEDICATED TO MILO K., THE MOST LOYAL, HONEST, PROUD, RESPECTFUL, FUNNY, ANGRY, OBNOXIOUS, RUDE, MANIPULATIVE HERMIT CRAB I'VE EVER MET.

IT IS ALSO DEDICATED TO FOUR CRUCIAL PEOPLE. TO MY WIFE, WENDY, WHO CONSTANTLY AMAZES ME WITH HER SUPPORT, ENCOURAGEMENT AND LOVE, AND WHO ALWAYS TELLS ME "YOU CAN DO IT." TO OUR SON, AIDAN, WHO EVERY DAY SEEMS TO BE EVEN MORE EXCITED AND HAPPY ABOUT HIS DAD'S WEIRDNESS AND THE FREAKY PROJECTS THAT RESULT. TO MY MOTHER, DR. YVONNE KAYE, WHO HAS CONSISTENTLY BEEN MY "BIGGEST FAN" SINCE THE MINUTE SHE FIRST SAW ME. AND TO FRANK QUATTRONE, WHO HAPPILY PUBLISHED MY FIRST "MILO K. HERMIT CRAB" COMIC STRIP AND KEPT IT RUNNING FOR 10 YEARS.

AND A MASSIVE THANK YOU ALSO TO JOE, RALPH AND JASON FROM ZENESCOPE ENTERTAINMENT, WHO GAVE ME THIS OPPORTUNITY AFTER ONLY A FEW DAYS OF BEING TIED TO CHAIRS AND STRUCK WITH BROOM HANDLES.

SILVER DRAGON BOOKS, INC.

Joe Brusha • President & Publisher
Jennifer Bermel • VP Business Affairs
Ralph Tedesco • Executive Editor
Anthony Spay • Art Director
Christopher Cote • Production Manager

silver dragon

Never Underestimate A Hermit Crab, July 2013. First Printing. Published by Silver Dragon Books Inc. an imprint of Zenescope Entertainment Inc., 433 Caredean Drive, Ste. C, Horsham, Pennsylvania 19044. Silver Dragon Books and its logos are ® and © 2013 Silver Dragon Books. all rights reserved. Never Underestimate A Hermit Crab, its logo and all characters and their likeness © and ™ Daniel Sean Kaye, and Silver Dragon Books, Inc. Any similarities to persons (living or dead), events, institutions, or locales are purely coincidental. No portion of this publication may be reproduced or transmitted, in any form or by any means, without the expressed written permission of Silver Dragon Books except for artwork used for review purposes. Printed in Canada.

W W W . S I L V E R D R A G O N B O O K S . C O M • F A C E B O O K . C O M / S I L V E R D R A G O N B O O K S

THIS IS A HERMIT CRAB.

NOW YOU MIGHT THINK THAT HERMIT CRABS JUST SIT IN THEIR SHELLS, IGNORING THE WORLD, NOT DOING MUCH OF ANYTHING.

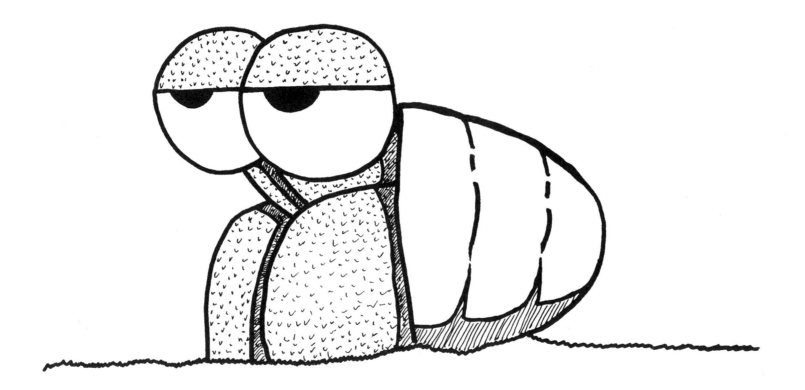

A LOT OF PEOPLE THINK THAT.

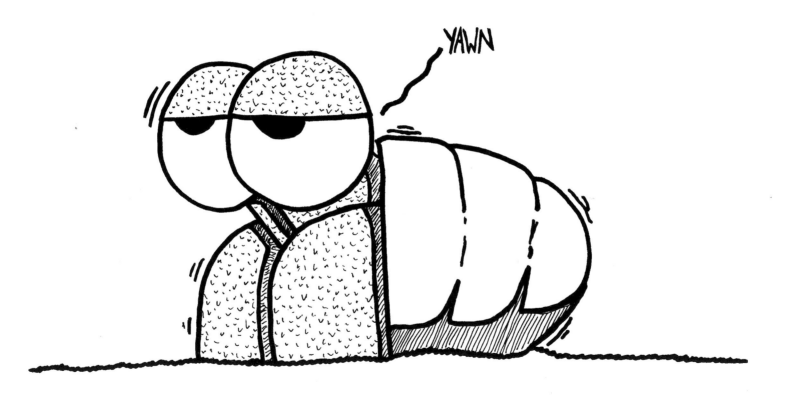

BUT THEY ARE WRONG.

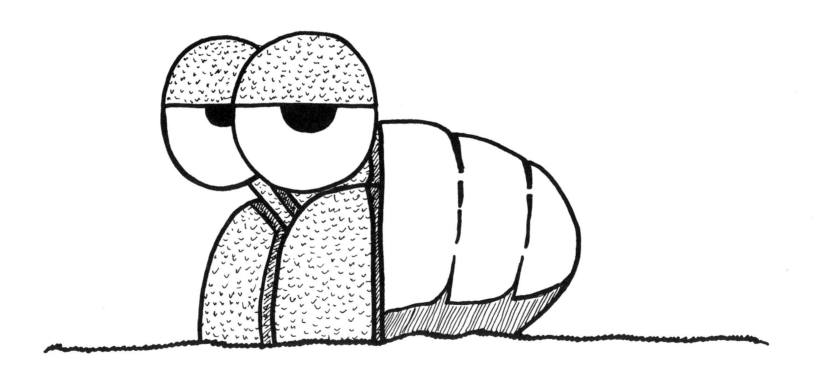

VERY, VERY WRONG...

FOR EXAMPLE, HERMIT CRABS
LOVE TO DANCE.

HERMIT CRABS OFTEN IMAGINE THEMSELVES AS ASTRONAUTS.

HERMIT CRABS OCCASIONALLY
RUN FOR OFFICE.

HERMIT CRABS DON'T DRIVE, BUT THEY THINK THEY LOOK GOOD WHILE SITTING IN CARS.

HERMIT CRABS TAKE KARATE,
BUT RARELY GET ABOVE
THEIR FIRST BELT.

HERMIT CRABS THINK THEY CAN CONTROL PEOPLE'S MINDS.

HERMIT CRABS LOVE COMIC BOOKS, ALTHOUGH THEY ARE VERY CRITICAL.

HERMIT CRABS KNOW ALL SORTS OF HOME IMPROVEMENT TECHNIQUES.

HERMIT CRABS ARE
GREAT STORYTELLERS.

HERMIT CRABS OFTEN GET DRESSED UP BECAUSE THEY FEEL FASHION IS FUN.

HERMIT CRABS LIKE TO IMAGINE
THE MOON IS MADE OF CHEESE.

HERMIT CRABS RARELY PICK UP
AFTER THEMSELVES.

HERMIT CRABS ARE AFRAID
OF SHADOWS.

HERMIT CRABS' FAVORITE HOLIDAYS ARE THEIR OWN BIRTHDAYS, WHICH OFTEN GET OUT OF CONTROL.

HERMIT CRABS HAVE VERY GOOD
SELF-IMAGES. (MAYBE TOO GOOD.)

SO THE NEXT TIME YOU THINK YOUR HERMIT CRAB IS JUST SITTING THERE, NOT DOING MUCH OF ANYTHING, REMEMBER THIS...

HERMIT CRABS CAN DO ALL SORTS OF THINGS....

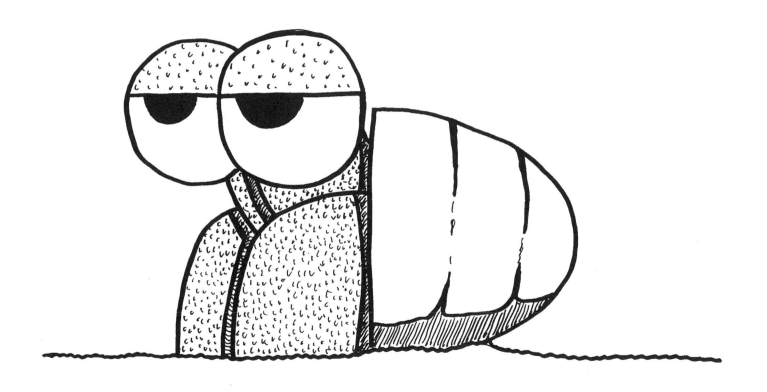

JUST LIKE YOU!

CARING FOR YOUR HERMIT CRAB

WHILE THIS BOOK IS SILLY FUN, CARING FOR YOUR HERMIT CRAB IS SERIOUS BUSINESS! IF YOU DO BRING ONE HOME, REMEMBER THESE IMPORTANT TIPS:

- KEEP THEM AT A TEMPERATURE BETWEEN 72°F AND 80°F.

- KEEP THEIR HABITAT AT A TROPICAL 70% TO 80% HUMIDITY.

- USE A 10-GALLON GLASS AQUARIUM—BIG ENOUGH TO HOLD FOOD AND WATER DISHES, EXTRA SHELLS (IMPORTANT FOR THEM TO HAVE DIFFERENT SIZES TO MOVE INTO) AND CLIMBING TOYS, WHILE GIVING THEM SPACE TO ROAM.

- GIVE THEM A LARGE NATURAL SPONGE IN A DISH WITH WATER IN IT.

- GIVE THEM A SUBSTRATE (SAND OR GRAVEL) DEEP ENOUGH TO BURY THEMSELVES, BUT SHALLOW ENOUGH SO THEY CAN FEEL THE UNDER-TANK HEATER'S WARMTH.

- LOW WATTAGE NIGHT-LIGHT BULBS ARE GOOD FOR HELPING YOUR CRAB BASK AND STAY ACTIVE (12 HOURS OF LIGHT AND 12 HOURS OF DARKNESS IS A GOOD IDEA).

THIS IS VERY BASIC INFORMATION, SO BE SURE TO RESEARCH FOR MORE DETAILED TIPS!